The Little Dancer

and
Other Stories

CONTENTS

STECK-VAUGHN®
C O M P A N Y
ELEMENTARY · SECONDARY · ADULT · LIBRARY

The Little Dancer

Tim was mad.
"It's not fair," he said.
"I want some dancing shoes.
I want to go to dancing lessons
just like Lisa."

"Your feet are too small,"
said Tim's mom.
"They don't make dancing shoes
for such small feet.
But you know, Tim, you don't need
lessons to dance.
Dance is everywhere."

Tim went into the garden.
The sun was shining on the grass.
It made the grass look silver and
then green.
"The sun is dancing," said Tim.
"I will dance a sun dance."
And he did.

A cloud went over the sky.
Then another floated gently by.
They changed shape.
"The clouds are dancing," said Tim.
"I will dance a cloud dance."
And he did.

Then the wind began to blow.
It shook the trees and
bent the grass.
"Now the wind is dancing," said Tim and
he danced a wild wind dance.

A few drops of rain began to fall.
Tim looked at the rain.
"Even the rain dances," he said and
began to dance a rain dance.
"Come inside, Tim," said his mom.
"You will get wet."

That night, Tim looked out
of his window.
He saw the stars in the sky.
"The stars are dancing, too," he said and
danced a spinning star dance into bed.
"You were right," Tim said to
his mom as he closed his eyes.
"Dance is everywhere."

The Special Pet

"I wish I had a puppy," said Jane.

"Puppies eat a lot," Mom said.

"It could eat my meat," said Jane.

She did not like meat.

"Sorry, Jane," said Mom.

Jane went into the yard.
She lay down on the grass.
She wished she had a puppy.
She looked at the long grass.
She saw the tips of
some white ears.

A white rabbit ran out.

It looked at Jane.

It let her pick it up.

She took it inside.

"This is my magic pet," she said.

"He was in the yard.

I will call him Snowdrop."

"We can't keep him," said Mom.
"He must belong to someone."
She put a note in the store.
FOUND, WHITE RABBIT.
Jane hoped nobody would come for him.

Then a mother and her little boy
came to the house.
"Yes, that's our rabbit,"
said the boy's mother.
"He got out and ran away."
The little boy smiled.
"Yes, that's Snowflake," he said.

Jane tried not to cry.
The rabbit would go now.
"We are moving to an apartment,"
said the boy's mother.
"There is no yard," she said.
"Ben can't keep his rabbit."
Ben looked very sad.

"Please, Mom," said Jane.

"Can we keep Snowdrop?"

"All right," said Mom.

Ben cried and Jane felt sorry for him.

"Let's share the rabbit," she said.

"Let's call him Snowy.

You can come and see him every day."

Ben was happy. He came every day.
He brought the rabbit's cage.
Ben and Jane let Snowy
run in the yard.
They saw the tips of his ears
above the long grass.
"Our special pet," said Jane.

The Bouncy Ball

Kate found a yellow ball.
She picked it up and took it home.
She bounced and bounced it.
Up it went.
It hit the ceiling, then the cat, then
bounced right through the open door.

Kate chased it as it bounced along.
She reached the gate but was too late.
The ball was gone.
She couldn't see it anywhere.

A van was outside the gate.
The driver climbed into it and
went off down the road.
That night he gave his son a ball.
"I found it in my van," he said.
"How it got there, I don't know."

"Thank you, Dad."
His son was pleased and
bounced the ball against a wall.
"Whoops! It's bouncy. Very bouncy!"
He bounced and bounced it.
Up it went, along the path and
bounced right over the garden wall.

In the train were Mom and Carla,
bored with sitting very still.
"Whoops! A ball. Look!" cried Carla.
"It came in through the open window."
Carla bounced it. Up it shot,
hit the ceiling, hit the floor, then
bounced right out through the window.

A truck was coming down the road,
loaded with all kinds of things:
crates of carrots, onions, apples,
pears, tomatoes – and the ball.

The light turned red.
The truck stopped.
The ball fell off.
One, two, three, it bounced
across the bridge and . . . .
"Whoops! A ball. Look!" cried Carlos.
"It fell right off that bridge up there."

After supper, in the park,
Carlos and his little brother
bounced the ball — and off it shot.
Down the path and through the park gates,
then it rolled slowly down the road.
"Here's my ball," said Kate surprised.
"The one I lost!"